Branded

Eric Walters

Orca currents

ORCA BOOK PUBLISHERS

For those who not only "talk the talk,"
but also "walk the walk."

Library and Archives Canada Cataloguing in Publication

Walters, Eric, 1957-

Branded / written by Eric Walters.

(Orca currents)

ISBN 978-1-55469-268-2 (bound).--ISBN 978-1-55469-267-5 (pbk.)

I. Title. II. Series: Orca currents

PS8595.A598B73 2010   jC813'.54   C2009-906834-6

First published in the United States, 2010
Library of Congress Control Number: 2009940769

Summary: Ian learns that the company that makes the uniforms for his
school is reputed to use child labor.

Orca Book Publishers gratefully acknowledges the support for its publishing
programs provided by the following agencies: the Government of Canada
through the Canada Book Fund and the Canada Council for the Arts,
and the Province of British Columbia through the BC Arts Council
and the Book Publishing Tax Credit.

Cover design by Teresa Bubela
Cover photography by Getty Images

Orca Book Publishers
PO Box 5626, Station B
Victoria, BC Canada
V8R 6S4

Orca Book Publishers
PO Box 468
Custer, WA USA
98240-0468

www.orcabook.com
Printed and bound in Canada.
Printed on 100% PCW recycled paper.
13 12 11 10 • 4 3 2 1

chapter one

"There are many causes for which I am prepared to die, but none for which I am prepared to kill," Mr. Roberts said. "Does anybody know who said that?"

"You, Mr. Roberts," Oswald said.

Some of the class laughed. Mr. Roberts silenced them with a look.

"I told you I pay more attention in class than you realize," Oswald said. "Even when my eyes are closed my mind is—"

Mr. Roberts aimed his look at Oswald and turned it up a half notch. That silenced Oswald midsentence.

Julia raised her hand. "It was Gandhi," she said, "political activist and the man who gained independence for India."

"Very good, Julia," he said. "But I expect nothing less from you."

"Thank you," she said.

Julia and Mr. Roberts had a very "polite" relationship. Considering how it all started between them, this was a major step forward.

Mr. Roberts had taken over as the new principal last semester. He wanted to make a whole lot of changes—changes that Julia, as the student president, thought it was her role to oppose. She tried to organize a schoolwide walkout in protest and called him "a stupid, mouth-breathing, chest-thumping ape" on Facebook. He suspended her for five days.

Even though they were polite—really polite—I got the feeling that Julia was waiting for an excuse to attack. Julia was like an elephant—she never forgot, especially something like a suspension. Before Mr. Roberts, she'd never even had a detention.

"Does anybody else wish to contribute something about Mahatma Gandhi?" Mr. Roberts asked.

I raised my hand, and Mr. Roberts nodded in my direction.

"Ian," he said.

"Gandhi defeated the English, who ruled India, by using passive resistance."

"What's that?" Oswald asked.

"He told people not to fight back against violence. He told his followers to absorb the blows but not strike out against those who were hitting them."

"A very hard thing to do," Mr. Roberts said. "Many people think it takes bravery to fight back, but it takes even more bravery to not fight back."

Oswald waved his hand in the air.

"Yes, Oswald?"

"I'm a little confused," said Oswald.

"A little?" Mr. Roberts asked and everybody, including Oswald, laughed.

Oswald and Mr. Roberts had a strange relationship. It wasn't particularly polite, but they both seemed to enjoy it.

"My apologies for the cheap shot," Mr. Roberts said. "No offence."

"Hey, no problem. I'm confused because you're talking about there being no cause worth killing for, but you were in the Marines...Didn't they sort of train you to fight back and try to kill people?"

Mr. Roberts chuckled. "They trained us to defend our country."

"And if that meant killing somebody?" Oswald asked.

"I would have done my duty."

I could imagine Mr. Roberts killing somebody. He probably wouldn't even need a weapon. He was an ex-Marine, but he still looked like a Marine. He was tall and stocky and had a crew cut. I wouldn't want to cross him—well, not again.

We'd had a clash in the beginning, but it's strange—I think he admired me for taking a stand against one of his policies.

"I greatly admire Gandhi," Mr. Roberts continued, "but I think there are some things for which we must be prepared to fight against, die for, and yes, kill."

"What sort of things?" Oswald asked.

"We need to fight oppression, terrorism and threats to our way of life, to protect democracy—"

"Didn't Gandhi create the largest democracy in the world by not fighting?" I asked, cutting him off.

"Yes, he did. You seem to know a great deal about Gandhi," Mr. Roberts said.

"I've been keeping up with the reading," I said.

Mr. Roberts's social justice class had caused me to read a whole lot of things that hadn't been assigned.

"Some people believe we should fight for what is right—even if that means breaking the law," Mr. Roberts said.

"It's the moral duty of somebody to disobey a law he doesn't agree with," I answered.

"Aaaah, now you're speaking the words of Dr. Martin Luther King," Mr. Roberts said. "It could be argued that Dr. King adopted Gandhi's principles and practices."

That opened up a whole discussion. Other students added opinions and quotes and arguments. This class often went way off the assigned topics, but that made it even better.

Besides, Mr. Roberts was the principal. He wasn't going to get in trouble for not following the course outline. In fact, he created this course and insisted on teaching it. He said he thought every principal should teach at least one course to "stay in touch" with his students.

Mr. Roberts was in constant touch with the students. He was always in the hallways, in the cafeteria, in the yard, at all the games and even at the school dances. He seemed to be everywhere. He didn't miss much. He seemed to know everything and everybody in the school.

Of course whether he knew you or not didn't matter if you were breaking any of the rules. And there were lots of rules to break. Mr. Roberts had added quite a few since he had become our principal. We weren't allowed hats, iPods or cell phones. There was to be no misbehavior, with no exceptions. He didn't like it when people broke rules or...I had an idea.

I raised my hand.

"Ian?"

"I was just wondering, if Gandhi didn't agree with your no-hat position, and he wore a hat to school would—"

"Gandhi did not wear a hat!" Julia said, cutting me off.

"I'm not saying he did, but suppose he wore a hat for, say, religious reasons, like Sikhs wear turbans or some Jewish people wear a yarmulke. What then?"

"That wouldn't be against the rules," Mr. Roberts said, "because it's part of their religion."

"Then I should be able to wear my Yankee's cap," Oswald said. "They are a religion to me."

"The Yankees are not a religion," Mr. Roberts said firmly. He paused, and a slight smile came to his face. "Now if you'd said the Boston Red Sox, you could have made an argument."

"Boston? You gotta be joking!" Oswald exclaimed. "I wouldn't wear a Red Sox cap on a—"

"Fine, fine, fine," I said, cutting him off. "Okay, so what if Gandhi wore a Red Sox cap?" I asked.

"Then his hat would be taken away," Mr. Roberts said.

"And if he refused to give up his hat?" I asked.

"Then he would be suspended," Mr. Roberts said.

"But Gandhi would only wear a hat because he thought it was right," I said.

"Regardless of his belief, I would have to follow my rules and suspend him."

"I can't believe that you'd suspend Gandhi," Oswald gasped.

"If he didn't follow the rules, it would be my unfortunate position to suspend him."

"And Gandhi would walk right up to you wearing that hat and dare you to suspend him," I said. "Defying the rule to raise awareness of its unjust nature."

"Yes, he would—"

The bell rang to end class, drowning out his last few words.

"That bell could wake the dead," Mr. Roberts said as it faded. "Please make sure you all attend the assembly," he said. "It is mandatory, and as you know I would give Gandhi a detention if he didn't show up!"

We had a school assembly once a week, and it was the same as any other class. If you didn't attend you were given a detention.

I joined Oswald and Julia. We started to leave with the rest of the class.

"Oswald!" Mr. Roberts called out. "Can you please stay after class? I want to discuss something with you."

Oswald nodded solemnly. This wasn't going to be good. Oswald hadn't handed in today's assignment. He was hoping that Mr. Roberts wouldn't notice. Fat chance. Mr. Roberts noticed everything.

I gave Oswald a tap on the shoulder. "Hang in there," I whispered.

"Do you think he's ever going to learn to keep his mouth shut?" Julia asked as we walked out of the class.

"How long have you known Oswald?" I asked.

"Fair enough. But he was just joking around in there. Mr. Roberts has to be a little understanding."

I laughed. "Remember, this is a guy who would suspend Gandhi. What chance does Oswald have? Besides, this isn't about what Oswald said, it's about him not handing in today's assignment."

"Did he really think he could get away with that?" Julia asked.

"He thought Mr. Roberts wouldn't notice, and he'd hand it in tomorrow."

"Not smart," Julia said. "But that's Oswald."

chapter two

I waited for Oswald at my locker. He never showed, so I was almost late for the assembly. The auditorium was nearly full when I walked in. That was no problem for me because the seat that I was heading for would be empty. I made my way to the front of the room in the very center. Julia was the only person sitting in the front row. Where was Oswald? I expected that he'd be there.

Hardly anybody else ever willingly sat up front. It wasn't my idea or Oswald's.

Julia said it was her responsibility as student president to be visible to all the students and staff.

I slumped into the seat beside her.

"Where's Oswald?" she asked.

"I was going to ask you the same thing. Maybe he lost track of time."

"He'd lose track of his head if it wasn't loosely attached to his body," she said.

"I just hope he gets here on time."

"You don't think..."

"He wasn't suspended," I said. "That's just crazy thinking."

"So crazy that you thought of it too without me saying it," said Julia.

"Mr. Roberts likes Oswald," I argued.

"He'd suspend Gandhi, remember? Oswald better get here soon. The assembly is about to start."

I looked at my watch. It was synced to school time, to the second. It was less than a minute to the start of the period, and that meant the assembly would start in one minute. Things always started on time since Mr. Roberts had become principal.

"I don't know what's worse, missing the assembly or walking in late," Julia said. "You know how Roberts is about people being late."

Julia said people and not students, because Mr. Roberts was no easier on staff who arrived late.

"From where we're sitting, it's not like Mr. Roberts won't notice Oswald isn't here either," I said, looking around. "Maybe he can sneak in and take a seat at the back."

The crowd noise suddenly stopped. I looked up to see Mr. Roberts striding across the stage. Everybody knew to shut up when he appeared. On stage, already seated, were the two vice-principals and the department heads. None of them were talking. They knew better too.

Mr. Roberts could be tough, but he was fair about it. When somebody else was at the podium talking, he listened, hands folded on his lap, paying complete attention.

"Good afternoon," Mr. Roberts said. "I'm so glad you all chose to join us this fine Friday afternoon."

"Like we had a choice," Julia said under her breath.

She always gave a running commentary—but never loud enough that Mr. Roberts would notice.

"I want to start by offering congratulations to our girls' volleyball team, which won the city championship!"

The crowd cheered and clapped and whistled. The applause slowly faded away.

"Now I'm going to announce another way that our school is going to lead the entire city. The school board has selected our school to pilot a new project."

"My guess is guard dogs or bars on the windows," Julia whispered out of the side of her mouth.

"This new change will help to improve security," Mr. Roberts continued.

Maybe the guard dogs weren't so far off.

"These changes will allow us to be more visible, not just at school but also in the community."

"My guess is fingerprints, mug shots or tattoos," she muttered.

I knew Mr. Roberts hated tattoos. This was strange since he had a tattoo on his arm. It was the Marine Corps emblem, an eagle sitting on top of the world. Once a Marine, always a Marine.

"Rather than simply telling you about our new change, I want to show you."

He gestured to the side, and Oswald walked onto the stage. He was wearing a jacket and a tie! I didn't even know Oswald owned a tie.

"Introducing our new school uniforms," Mr. Roberts announced.

There was a stunned silent reaction from the audience. It was as if no one could believe what they'd heard or seen.

"He didn't just say uniforms, did he?" Julia asked loudly.

In the silence of the auditorium her words carried across the room. They triggered a response, and people started to talk and groan. There were even some boos.

Mr. Roberts raised his hands in the air and the noise lessened, but it didn't stop completely.

"Your attention, please!" he barked, and the room fell silent again. "Oswald has the honor of being the first student at our school to wear the new uniform."

Oswald was obviously being punished in a very public way. He looked uncomfortable. Oswald liked being the center of attention, but this was too much attention in too central a spot.

"It is a simple uniform," said Mr. Roberts. "Black pants, white shirt, blazer and tie. The green sweater Oswald is wearing is optional. The sweater and the blazer feature our school crest."

"We have a school crest?" I whispered to Julia.

"Of course we do."

"Starting next semester," said Mr. Roberts, "which you all know begins in three weeks, we will become the first public high school in our city to wear uniforms."

This time there was an instant reaction and the booing became a larger part of the mix.

Mr. Roberts had to raise his voice to silence the crowd.

"Now, are there any questions?" he asked. It seemed like he was looking directly at me—no, he was looking at Julia.

Julia jumped to her feet.

"Why wasn't the student council consulted about this decision?" she demanded.

"There are many things which are beyond the scope of student council, but in this case, things just moved so quickly that there wasn't time."

"How fair is it that students are expected to wear a uniform when some of your staff dress like they're going to the beach?" she asked.

We all knew which teachers she was talking about—although recently they had been dressing more formally.

"You make a valid point," Mr. Roberts agreed. "As we all know, some members of my staff have, in the past, dressed in a highly unprofessional manner. This has been corrected."

I looked up on the stage. The head of the English department was wearing a tie. The only way he would have worn a tie before was wrapped around his head like a headband.

"The new uniforms will be worn by all members of this school, including teachers and administration—as they were informed in a staff meeting prior to our assembly."

There was no reaction from the teachers on stage. Some of them had to be unhappy, but they sat there stone still.

"There are many reasons this decision was made, and I hope to have the opportunity to discuss this with you over the course of the next few weeks." He paused. "It's now the end of the day. You are dismissed."

On cue, the bell sounded. Kids jumped to their feet and started out of the auditorium. Julia rushed up to the stage, and I trailed behind. I didn't want to miss what she was going to say.

"Mr. Roberts!" she yelled. "We have to talk, right now!"

He looked down at her. "My office. Two minutes."

She nodded in agreement.

"And Ian, you come too," he said.

chapter three

We settled into chairs—Julia, myself and Oswald, who was still wearing the new school uniform. On the short trip from the auditorium, we'd been bombarded by people complaining about the uniforms. Most of the students thought they were unfair and asked Julia what she was going to do. There were threats that kids weren't going to take this lying down.

I knew Julia was about ready to burst. This was looking like the opportunity to take a stand against the principal that she had been waiting for.

Mr. Roberts closed the door to his office, sealing us in. He took a seat behind his desk. It was enormous. There were lots of papers on it, but it was very organized. Each pile of paper was neatly stacked and labeled.

"I assume that you are not in favor of the uniforms," he said.

"I'm completely opposed to them!" Julia thundered. "It's not fair!"

"Not fair?" Mr. Roberts questioned. "The concept of fairness involves conformity to standards in which all people are treated equally. How is this not fair?"

Julia opened to mouth to speak, but nothing came out. She looked helpless. I needed to do something.

"Maybe she chose the wrong word," I said. "Since everybody is going to wear the uniforms—"

"Including the teachers and myself," Mr. Roberts added.

"Yeah, including all the staff makes it fair, but maybe it isn't the right thing to do," I said.

"And how do you think it is wrong, Ian?"

"I really, you know, don't know if it is wrong," I sputtered.

"You think this is a good idea?" Julia asked angrily as she turned to face me.

"I didn't say that either!" I said.

"So you do think this is a mistake," Mr. Roberts asked.

I felt myself stuck between a rock and a hard place...no, that would have been better.

"I only came because you asked me to come. I didn't really..." Julia was growing angrier by the second. "But I'm glad I'm here now. I want to hear both sides of this argument. I really do."

I really didn't.

"Good. An open mind is a good thing," said Mr. Roberts. "Let me start by explaining the reasoning behind this decision.

"The concept of uniforms is based on a sense of equality. You all know how students use clothing to define status. Rich kids wear the most expensive designer clothes."

"And those who can't afford them struggle to keep up," I added.

"Exactly," Mr. Roberts said.

I worked at not looking at Julia because I knew I wouldn't like the look she'd give me. She had in the past accused me of being the "principal's pet." I was nobody's pet, including hers.

"Uniforms cost money," Julia said. "What about those who can't afford them? They're not free."

"They cost less money than regular clothing," Mr Roberts answered. "And we have worked out an arrangement where all students will receive uniforms at a reduced price. For those who still cannot afford them, they are free."

So much for that argument.

"If you think about it logically, between gym clothes with the school name on them, team uniforms and the dress code we already have, this isn't a giant leap," Mr. Roberts added.

Julia looked like she wanted to say something, but she didn't know what to say.

"There is also the safety factor," Mr. Roberts continued. "The uniforms will allow us to quickly identify who belongs here and who doesn't. That makes it safer for all the students. You do want the students to be safe, don't you, Julia?"

"Yes, of course."

"Then you can see why the uniforms are, in fact, not only fair but also a good idea."

Julia nodded her head ever so slightly in agreement.

I had to hand it to him. Mr. Roberts had all the answers, and Julia was completely unprepared. Is that why he'd called us down right away, why he'd sprung it on everybody like this? Was this a sneak attack? A Marine would know all about sneak attacks.

"Oswald, you've been uncharacteristically quiet," Mr. Roberts said.

"It might be the uniform. Maybe it's having a positive effect on me already, like medication to control my normal hyperactivity."

"I can only dream," Mr. Roberts said. He and Oswald reached across the table and gave each other a little low five.

"I meant, what do you think about the uniform?" he asked.

"It's a little stiff, but I guess it'll soften up as I wear it. The tie feels a bit like a noose."

"Stand up," Mr. Roberts said.

Oswald got to his feet. Mr. Roberts stood and leaned across the desk to adjust Oswald's necktie.

"Is that better?"

"Much," Oswald said. "I think, all in all, this won't be the worst thing in the world, at least for me." He turned to face me. "But I'm a little worried about Ian, here."

"Me?"

"Yeah, on me, this really works, but I don't know if you have the basic cool to pull it off," said Oswald. "On you it might look a little geeky, that's all."

I couldn't help but laugh.

"But don't worry, Ian, you just keep hanging around with me and you'll benefit from the cool halo that surrounds me," Oswald said, gesturing to himself.

"If that's why people hang out with you," I said, "then you'd be a pretty lonely guy, standing alone in your polyester jacket and—"

"Polyester blend," Oswald said, cutting me off. "See here." He opened the jacket up to reveal a label. "It's eighty-five-percent polyester and fifteen-percent cotton. So, like, fifteen percent of it is one-hundred-percent natural."

"You'll have to excuse me now," Mr. Roberts said. "I have a few more hours of work to do before the day is done, and I'm sure the three of you are anxious to start your weekend."

We thanked him and left his office. I closed the door behind me.

"Thanks a lot," Julia said.

"Sure, no problem," Oswald said.

"I was being sarcastic," she said.

"Really?" Oswald replied, leaving no doubt that he was being sarcastic.

"Could you at least take off that stupid uniform?" she asked.

"No can do. I know for a fact it's against the present dress code to walk around in my boxers. Although I could pull off that look too."

"Just shut up and go and get changed back to your regular clothes," I said. "We'll wait for you at the back door."

chapter four

We sat on the wall and waited for Oswald.
A steady stream of kids came up and told
us how upset they were about the uniforms.
It looked like a very unpopular decision.

All the commotion had a plus and a
minus. Having other people around meant
I didn't have to talk to Julia. That was
good. The downside was that they gave her
more ammunition. I really wasn't looking
forward to the ride home. If it wasn't so
far, I might have thought about walking.

It was Julia's car, so it wasn't like I could leave without her.

I had the strangest thought—I could ask to borrow the keys because I wanted to wait in the car. Then I'd just drive away. If she was angry now, I could just picture her face when I honked, waved out the window and drove away in her car. It almost would have been worth it.

Oswald came out of the school.

"Let's go," I said to Julia.

"Hang on," she said. She turned back to the three girls she was talking to. "I don't know what we're going to do, but we'll do something about those uniforms," she reassured them.

Oh, great, she was going to do something. That, of course meant she'd want me and Oswald to do something with her.

I motioned for Oswald to come with me, and we left her behind. We walked across the parking lot and sat on the hood of Julia's little red Neon. It sagged under our weight.

"Look, whatever you do, don't say yes to anything Julia suggests on the way home," I said.

"What if she suggests stopping at Wendy's and buying us both a number one combo, her treat?"

"She's not going to suggest that. And even if she did, that would only be a bribe to get us to go along with her."

"I'm open to bribes," Oswald suggested. "But if she thinks she can get me to do something crazy for a meal, she's the one who's crazy."

"Good, because—"

"I'll hold out for at least three meals," he said. "Or maybe it should be pro-rated. Two meals for each detention it costs me and four meals for each day of suspension."

"Quit joking around."

"I'm not joking. If she crosses Mr. Roberts on this, detentions and suspensions are definitely on the menu," Oswald replied.

"Just don't agree with her," I said. I thought about how that might just get her going even more. "And don't disagree with her either."

Oswald laughed. "That narrows down the options. What are you suggesting?"

"Let's just try to be neutral, not commit, not get involved, but not *not* get involved. Let's wait her out until she gets calmer."

"Does waiting her out ever work?" Oswald asked. "She just gets more revved up. Maybe we should just make a run for it and...too late. Here she comes."

Julia walked toward us. I expected her to look angry, but she didn't. Instead there was a smug little smirk on her face. She was enjoying this or was amused by it. Julia angry was dangerous. Julia amused was deadly.

She clicked her remote, and the car beeped and the locks clicked up. She climbed in, and I did a loop around Oswald and opened the back door. I gave him a little smile. He knew what I was doing and why I was doing it. Usually we would have fought for the front seat, but not today. I would have taken the trunk if I could have gotten away with it. Oswald climbed in beside Julia. What choice did he have?

I slid across the backseat so I was directly behind Julia. That way she couldn't even see me in the rearview mirror.

Julia started the car, and we drove away. So far there was silence. Silence was good. Thirty seconds down and about five hundred to go, as long as we made all the lights and there was no traffic.

"So what are we going to do?" Julia asked.

I didn't answer. I knew I could wait, and Oswald would fill the silence.

"What are we going to do about what?" Oswald asked.

"Are you stupid?" she snapped.

"Well, that's another question completely. Are we going to do something about me being stupid? Is that what you mean?"

"There's nothing that can be done about that, short of surgery or a miracle drug," Julia said.

"I know enough to 'just say no to drugs.' Are you talking about the uniforms?" he asked.

"Of course I'm talking about the uniforms. What are we going to do?"

"That's easy," Oswald said. "We're going to get those uniforms and put them on and then go to school. I'm looking forward to seeing you in one of those uniforms."

"What?" Julia questioned.

"Yeah, I saw pictures of the girls' uniform. Knees socks and short skirts and—"

"Shut up, Oswald."

"And if you wore high heels, it would—"

"Do you want to walk?" Julia asked.

"Not really, but at least I'm wearing running shoes instead of high heels."

"Shut up, Oswald. Ian, what are we going to do?" Julia asked.

"I'm thinking," I replied. Of course, what I was thinking about was how much it would hurt if I jumped out of the moving car. Probably about the same pain as if I stayed.

"And do you have any ideas?" she asked.

"I'm working on eliminating ideas," I answered.

"And what does that mean?"

"It means that we should rule certain things out. Things like posting nasty comments about Mr. Roberts on Facebook or threatening a boycott of school."

Oswald snickered. "You've been there, done that, got the suspension."

"I wasn't planning to do any of those things," she said. "Unlike some people in this car, I learn from my mistakes."

"Hey, hey, I object to that comment!" Oswald said. "I eventually learn from my mistakes...and then move on to bigger, more interesting mistakes. You should both be grateful for what I do. I consider myself a role model."

"Wanna explain that one?" I asked.

"What's to explain? You learn from good examples and bad examples. You both have to admit that you have learned from my adventures."

"No argument there," Julia agreed. "So, Ian, what if we do one of those flash-mob things that you and Oswald like so much?"

"We haven't done one of those in months," I said.

"Then this is the perfect time to do one."

"I thought you didn't like flash mobs, that you thought they were stupid," Oswald said.

"I did think they were stupid until the one that got back the school dances."

Flash mobs were sudden gatherings of people, designed most often to do something silly like a pillow fight, or a mass coughing, or singing a song.

I'd organized a lunchtime flash mob in which every student in the school gathered, listened to their iPods and silently danced. That had convinced Mr. Roberts to allow us to have school dances again because everybody was so well-behaved.

"And just how do you think this flash mob would work?" I asked. "What would people do?"

"I think they should all take off their school uniforms and stand around naked," Oswald suggested.

I laughed. "I don't know if I would be willing to participate, but I'd certainly be willing to film that and post it on YouTube.

That would get a couple of million views really fast."

"Please be serious," she said.

"He is being serious, that *would* get millions of views," Oswald said. "Depending on who he has the camera focused on, I might watch that one a million times myself."

Julia pulled into my driveway. I was so grateful to be getting out first.

"Thanks for the ride," I said.

"Could you at least think about it?" Julia asked.

"Sure, I'll think," I said. I just couldn't promise to come up with an answer.

chapter five

My phone vibrated in my pocket, and my mother gave me a disapproving look. She didn't like us to take phone calls during meals. She had nothing to worry about. I wasn't going to answer it.

I pulled out the phone and turned it off.

"Thank you," she said.

"You're welcome."

"Who was it?" my father asked.

"I didn't look," I said. I didn't look because I was pretty sure who it was.

"You figure it's Julia?" he asked.

"Probably." She'd already called me three times—once on the home phone—since she'd dropped me off. She was relentless.

"Is something bothering her?" my mother asked.

"Something's always bothering her."

"You will call her back, right?" my mother asked. "It's only polite."

"I will. Just not right now. It wouldn't be polite to interrupt our meal."

"You should invite her for dinner more often," my mother said.

"At least then she wouldn't call during the meal," I said.

"I really do like that girl," she said.

"I don't."

"You don't? But...you're putting me on," she said.

"Of course I like her, she's one of my best friends," I said.

"You know, I can still see the two of you together as a couple," she said.

"Leave the boy alone," my father said.

I know he had the same thoughts, but he was smart enough to keep them to himself.

"You two would make such a cute couple," she went on.

"Julia isn't the sort of person you date," I said.

"No?" my mother asked.

"But marriage I could see," I said.

"What?" both my parents said in unison.

"Julia would be a nightmare to date," I explained. "She's too opinionated, too temperamental and too difficult—at least right now. But later, like after university, I think she might mellow out."

"I guess that could happen," my father said.

"What did you think of Mom when you first met her?" I asked.

He laughed. I thought I already knew the answer. They had met when they were both beginning lawyers. They were on opposite sides of a trial, battling against each other.

"Well, what did you think of her?" I asked again.

"To be honest, I thought she was opinion-ated, temperamental, difficult and—"

"Look who's talking!" she exclaimed.

"Let me finish," he said. "And she was so hot that I could hardly keep my mind on the trial."

My mother leaned over and gave my father a big kiss.

"Come on now, no public displays of affection...I'm trying to eat here!"

They stopped their little lip-lock. My father actually looked embarrassed.

"It's nice to know that you and Julia have a future together," my mother said.

"Don't start planning the wedding right now," I said.

"No plans. So what does Julia want to talk to you about?" she asked.

"She's all upset about our new school uniforms," I said.

"Your school is getting uniforms?" my mother asked.

"Not yet. Next semester."

"This is news to us," my father said. "Why didn't you tell us about it?"

"It was sprung on us by Mr. Roberts today."

"Not surprising that he'd want uniforms," my father said. "He does like things to be orderly and organized."

"And Julia objects to the uniforms?" my mother asked.

"Oh yeah, definitely."

"Does she have some plan to fight them?" she asked.

"I think her plan mainly involves getting me to come up with something."

Both my parents looked concerned.

"You're not planning an Internet campaign or a flash mob, are you?" my mother asked.

"We don't want you to do anything stupid," my father added.

"Generally I leave stupid up to Oswald. Always good to let an expert handle things. Me, I'm not planning anything. I don't even think there's anything that wrong with school uniforms."

"I can't imagine wearing the same thing to work every day," my father said.

"Really?" I asked. "Don't you wear a dark suit, white shirt, dress pants and a tie almost every day?"

"But that's not a uniform," he said.

"Your suits are all black or dark blue. Your ties are almost all red or blue patterns. If you threw on a school crest, you would be wearing our uniform."

"There are some benefits to a uniform, I imagine," my mother said.

"Mr. Roberts says that they're cheaper than regular clothes, that it makes everybody equal and that it provides for greater security."

"But Julia doesn't see it that way," my mother commented.

"What are her specific objections?" my father asked.

"I don't know if she has any specific objections. It's more like the principle of the matter. She hates to be told to do anything. You know about that sort of person," I answered and gestured toward my mother.

"Hey, hey, none of that!" she said playfully.

"So you do have a problem with the school uniforms," my father said.

"No, I don't."

"Yes, you do," he repeated. "Your problem is Julia expects you to do something."

"I guess that is a problem," I agreed.

"You know the best thing would be to just tell her that you're okay with the uniforms," my mother said.

"I don't see that happening. I'm just going to humor her for a while and let her run out of steam. I don't know why she's so upset. It's really not that big a deal. In lots of countries, kids have to walk miles to get to school, or only the rich can afford to go," I said.

"It doesn't seem fair," my mother said, "that we have so much and so many have so little."

"Some of the stuff I'm learning in Mr. Roberts's class is unbelievable," I said.

"It seems like you're getting a lot out of that class," my father added. "You're always talking about it."

"It's a good class, and he's a really good teacher." I paused. "I think it's even helped me to make up my mind what profession I might pursue."

They both waited.

"I'm thinking it wouldn't be that bad to be a lawyer."

My father clapped his hands and my mother beamed. "That's wonderful!" she exclaimed.

Both my parents were lawyers—as was my sister, my older brother and a bunch of other relatives. I knew they wanted me to become a lawyer too. I'd always said I was going to be anything but a lawyer.

"And we owe this to Mr. Roberts and his class on social justice...right?"

"Yeah, he opened my eyes to what's going on in the world. There are lots of places where things aren't fair, where there isn't justice."

"And being a lawyer would help bring about justice," my father said proudly.

"Some lawyers do bring about justice," I agreed. "I could fight for human rights, maybe work for an agency that's trying to help people."

"That is wonderful," my mother said.

"But that's a long way off," I said. "First I have to worry about Julia and this uniform thing. You know, in half the countries in the world kids would be thrilled to get a uniform and be able to go to school. Instead, she's all upset."

"Maybe you could explain it to her just like that," my mother suggested.

"I could," I said, "but then you'd have to put those wedding plans on hold permanently."

chapter six

I opened my locker and put my gym bag inside. There was a loud thud as Oswald tossed his team uniform, shorts, socks and shoes—in one wet ball—into the bottom of his locker beside mine.

He and I were on the basketball team... well, on the bench on the team. We were both good enough to make the team but not good enough to get any serious playing time. The only time we worked up a real sweat was at practices.

Oswald's stuff had the odor of rotting compost.

"Are you planning to take that home to wash anytime soon?" I asked.

"When the basketball season is over," he said.

"The season still has weeks to go."

"And during those weeks my plan will become more effective," he said.

"And that plan is?"

"If I can't break an ankle with my crossover, I can at least knock them over with the smell," he said. "Would you want to cover me?"

"Point taken."

I saw Julia coming down the hall. I'd promised her I'd think some more, because last night I hadn't been able to come up with a plan. I still hadn't.

"I've been doing a lot of research about school uniforms," Julia said.

"How about saying, 'Hello, how are you?'"

"Sure, fine. Hello, how are you? I've been doing a lot of research about school uniforms," she repeated.

I didn't want to know, but I also knew what the correct response was.

"So what did you find out?" I asked.

"Well, almost every single point that Mr. Roberts made has an opposite argument," she said.

"For example?" I asked.

"Even if everybody wears the same uniform, there are other ways that students set themselves apart from each other, including hairstyles or strange colors, makeup..."

"So I guess that means that I'm going to have to start dying my hair," Oswald joked.

"Or putting on makeup and wearing jewelry," I added.

"Or wearing a fancy watch, or smoking, or something like that," Julia added.

"I'm sorry, but don't people smoke because they want to fit in, not stand out?" I questioned.

"Uniforms are just like smoking," she said.

"Do you want to explain that one to me?" I asked.

"That's easy," Oswald said. He reached into his locker and pulled out the uniform

jacket and put it on. "When I'm wearing
this, I'm smoking hot."

I laughed. Julia looked like she'd bitten
into something bad tasting. Maybe she'd
caught wind of his gym stuff.

"Which reminds me, I have to go get
changed," Oswald said.

"What?"

"I'm going to change into the new school
threads," he said. He pulled a pair of black
pants, a white shirt and the tie out of his
locker.

"Are you insane?" Julia demanded.

"That's not what my imaginary psychiatrist tells me."

"I think you need a real psychiatrist,"
Julia said.

"He's real to me," Oswald protested.
"Him and my imaginary friend, Ian, here.
I know you can't see him, but he's real and
his name is Ian and—"

"Just give me a normal answer. Why
would you put on that uniform when you
don't have to?" she asked.

"Simple. Haven't you heard that females love a man in uniform?"

"First off, that would be a man, not a boy, and second...well...no," she said, shaking her head.

"Oswald, are you really going to put that on?" I asked.

"Have to. Mr. Roberts told me to."

"He ordered you to put on that uniform?" Julia demanded.

"Not so much ordered as suggested. He said I could wear it and get marks for his course. It would be like an extra assignment. And believe me, I could use the marks."

Nobody would argue with that. Oswald walked away.

"And they don't really save money," Julia said, hardly skipping a beat.

"What?" I asked.

"Uniforms don't save money."

"How can they not save money?" I asked. "Even if we paid for them—and lots of people are getting them for free—

they are still cheaper than designer clothes by a long shot."

"That's assuming that kids will wear them all the time," she said. "Don't you think they're still going to need other clothes for after school or weekends? They're still going to buy the regular clothes. The uniforms are an extra cost."

She had a point—one that I hadn't thought of.

"Maybe you should mention that to Mr. Roberts," I suggested.

"Oh, I'll mention it to him." She paused. "But not right now."

"Why not?"

She leaned in close. "I'm not going to talk to him until I have everything thought out and in place," she said quietly. "He's not the only one who can plan an ambush. He won't even see it coming."

"See what coming?" I asked anxiously.

"I don't know yet, but I've never seen so many people upset." She paused and looked directly at me. "But you don't seem to be one of them. Do you like the idea of uniforms?"

"No, of course not," I said. Actually I didn't like or dislike the idea. It wasn't the big deal Julia was making it out to be.

"So I'm counting on you to come up with something. Are you sure a flash mob wouldn't work? It worked so well to get back the school dances."

"I can't see how to make it work against uniforms."

"Maybe everybody could show up off school property and be in regular clothing instead of the uniforms," she suggested.

"Well, we're allowed to wear regular clothing when we leave school so that won't be much of a protest."

"Oh yeah, right. But keep thinking, okay?"

"Sure, I'll keep thinking."

"And you can't tell Mr. Roberts anything about my plans," she said.

"That's easy. You don't have a plan."

"You can't even tell him that I'm trying to figure out a plan."

"No problem, but I wouldn't be surprised if he finds out anyway."

She gave me a questioning look.

"It won't be from me!" I protested. "But you know he doesn't miss much."

"Oh, he won't miss this," Julia said. "He just won't see it coming until it smacks him right in the face. Keep thinking about what that plan will be."

What I was going to think of the most was how to avoid getting myself in trouble. And maybe how to stop Julia from getting in trouble too. Keeping me out of trouble might be hard. The second part, keeping Julia safe, was going to be much harder.

chapter seven

I settled into my desk. Oswald was beside me, wearing his uniform. There was a mustard stain on the bottom of his left pant leg, and the knot on his tie was looking pretty strange. Julia hadn't arrived yet, and the bell was about to ring. She was probably busy talking to somebody about the uniforms. She'd spent the whole day trying to get people more upset about them than they were. She'd been so busy that she hadn't even had lunch with us. The good part about that was we didn't have to talk to her about any of it.

Julia rushed through the door as the bell rang—almost late, but on time.

"Sorry," she said to Mr. Roberts as she sat down on the other side of me.

"On time is on time," Mr. Roberts replied. "Let's get down to business. Could somebody turn off the lights?"

Josh jumped to his feet and flicked off the lights. It was completely dark until my eyes adjusted to the light coming through the blinds. A beam of light shot out from the digital projector and onto the screen.

It was a YouTube clip. Music started up as we looked at a dark screen. I recognized the music, but I couldn't place it. Wait—it was from a running-shoe commercial, but I couldn't remember which one. The screen shifted to an ad featuring one of my favorite basketball players. Underneath was written the amount of the endorsement money he got. It was more money than most people would earn in a lifetime! His picture faded to reveal a football star—one of those guys known by only his first name. He wasn't making as much money as the basketball star, but it was still a small fortune. That changed to a famous golfer—like that was a real sport. But he was being paid real money to wear those shoes when he wandered around the golf course. With that amount of money he could buy his own golf course—on his own island.

After the sports celebrities, the screen showed numbers—money, really big money!

"Wow," Oswald said, "that is a whole lot of zeroes."

It read *$15,000,000,000—Profit*. That was a lot of money for a company. Heck, that was a lot of money for a small country.

The image changed to a factory with long assembly lines. There were workers all along the line and shoes rolling down the conveyor belt. The camera panned down the assembly line and stopped at one of the workers—she looked awfully young. More words came across the screen.

Six cents an hour...seventy-two cents a day...six days a week...to earn $4.32 *a week. That's what this thirteen-year-old girl gets to make the shoes that THEY endorse...that YOU wear...Just think about it the next time you slip on those shoes.*

The little girl with sad eyes on the assembly line was replaced by shots of kids about my age playing sports. There were kids playing basketball and another group of kids playing football, and there was a shot of a whole schoolyard filled with kids.

The closing text said, *She works like a slave so that you can play.*

The clip faded and the lights came back on. I became aware of the logo on the shoes I was wearing. Thank goodness I was wearing a different brand today. Not that I didn't own a pair of those shoes, but they weren't my favorites.

"Comments?" Mr. Roberts asked.

"That was incredibly sad," Rachel said. "That poor girl."

"That isn't much of a life...does she really work that hard?"

"Six days a week," Mr. Roberts said. He paused. "At least that's what it said on the screen. By a show of hands, how many people think it's true?"

Most of the hands in the class went up.

"How many think it's just made up?" he asked.

A couple of hands went up—sort of.

"And how many people, really, don't know if it's true or not?"

Now more than half the hands, including mine, went up.

"That may be the cautious response," he said. "Those who believe it is not true, please explain the reason for your doubts."

"There's no way kids that young work in factories," Josh said. "That's illegal."

"It's illegal in this country," Mr. Roberts said. "We have child labor laws, but most developing countries either have no such laws or allow them to be ignored."

"But still," Josh continued. "Nobody would actually be paid six cents an hour... would they?"

"They would," Mr. Roberts said. "Now those who think this clip portrays the truth, please explain why."

"I've seen that clip before," Julia said. "And others like it."

"I've heard about that sort of thing as well," Courtney agreed. "Everybody knows those companies use sweatshops and child labor."

"And you know this how?" Mr. Roberts asked.

"It's just that everybody knows it," Courtney said, "sort of like how the sky is blue and—"

"Actually the sky isn't blue," Mr. Roberts said. "Any other explanations to support the truth of those statements?"

"Sports stars do get huge amounts of money for endorsements, and those guys do wear that brand of shoes," Oswald said.

"So we know that part of it is true."

"And that company does make lots of money," I added.

"True enough. So we know that some of what that YouTube clip contains is true. But you all should know that the best way to lie is to tell half the truth."

"And if you're doing that, you should probably include information that we know is true so that we assume the rest is true," I said.

"Exactly, Ian, exactly!" Mr. Roberts said.

"So, are you saying that that stuff isn't true?" Oswald asked.

"I'm not saying that," said Mr. Roberts.

"Are you saying it's true then?"

"I'm not saying that either. Can anyone give me another reason to believe that this clip is true?" Mr. Roberts asked. "Ian, any thoughts?"

"Well, I'm willing to bet that all of the numbers, all of the facts are true."

"Why would you think that?"

"Because if they weren't true, the company would sue or have the clip taken off YouTube," I said.

"That is good critical thinking, but as we all know, it's not wise to believe everything. Especially today." He paused. "In the olden days—when I was younger—information was generally printed in reference books like an encyclopedia."

"Not stone tablets?" Oswald asked.

Everybody laughed, including Mr. Roberts.

"We had paper. Something being written on paper didn't guarantee that it was true or that it wasn't biased, but it was generally written by some sort of expert. It's a lot different today."

"Any idiot can put something up on Wikipedia," Oswald said. "I know this for a fact, because I've put stuff on Wikipedia."

"Actually, they have found that Wikipedia is fairly accurate, but you're right," said Mr. Roberts. "Just because something is on YouTube or Twitter or on a Facebook page doesn't make it true."

I thought he deliberately avoided looking at Julia when he said that.

"Is it just that brand of shoes?" Oswald asked. He held up a foot to reveal the familiar logo.

"Not just that shoe brand. They just focused on that name for that clip. They could have done any shoe on the market."

I tucked my feet farther in under my desk.

"And it's not just running shoes of course. Most toys, electronics, household products, cleaning supplies and clothing are all potentially manufactured in sweatshops. It can be anything," Mr. Roberts said.

"This is starting to smell like an assignment," Oswald said.

"No assignment. Critical thinking should be a part of your lives. Doesn't anybody just want to know?"

A few hands went up, including mine.

"When something interests you, it drives you to find more information. We are in the information age. Just remember, be a critical thinker. Don't accept without proof. And on that note, I'm going to dismiss you."

"But the period isn't over," Oswald said.

"Do you want to stay longer?" he asked.

"No, I'm good with leaving!" Oswald said as he jumped to his feet. Other people started gathering their books.

"Actually I have to leave a little early. I have a meeting at the board office about the uniforms. And speaking of uniforms, Oswald, come here."

Oswald went to the front.

"Didn't anybody ever teach you how to tie a tie?"

"No, sir."

"It looks more like a noose than a necktie," Mr. Roberts said. He adjusted the tie so it looked better.

More than half of the class had already made for the door. I think they were afraid he might change his mind. That might not be the dumbest thing to do. I grabbed my things and—

"Ian," Mr. Roberts called out, and I froze in the doorway—two feet shy of freedom.

"Can I have a moment of your time?" he asked.

I knew that wasn't really a question.

I turned around and headed back into the class. I passed Julia, and she gave me a "What is this about?" look. I shrugged. How would I know what he wanted?

I stood beside his desk. He was shuffling papers and didn't even look up at me. I got the feeling he was waiting until the room emptied completely before he talked. It got very quiet as the last people exited, leaving just me and him.

He looked up. "Are you planning to do some independent investigation into the things we've talked about today?"

"For sure," I said.

"You really have impressed me with your interest in social justice."

"There's so much I didn't know."

"And so much you still don't know," he said.

"I didn't mean I know everything...I just mean I'm trying to learn more."

"We're all trying to learn. I was thinking about creating a social justice club here at the school," he said. "Would you be interested in taking a leadership role in that?"

"Yeah, of course."

"We'll try to make the student population aware of world issues. We'll try to think globally and act locally," he said.

I wasn't sure what that meant, but I figured I'd learn that too.

"So, changing subjects, what do you think about the new uniforms?" Mr. Roberts asked.

I hadn't seen that coming.

"I'm not asking for state secrets," he said. He must have read something in my expression. "I just want to know your opinion."

"They're just uniforms," I said. "No big deal."

"From what I gather a lot of people think it is a big deal."

"Some people make a big deal out of nothing," I said.

"And some people make nothing out of a big deal," he responded.

"What?"

"Sometimes things that really do matter aren't seen as being important. The secret is to know what counts and what doesn't," Mr. Roberts explained. "Speaking of which, I better get to the board office."

chapter eight

"Are you going to turn in soon?" my mother asked as she peeked in the door of my room.

"Soon. And you?"

"Possibly not so soon. I have a big day tomorrow, pre-trial hearing."

"I've been looking at situations where people need a good lawyer," I said.

"Really?" she said. She came into the room and looked over my shoulder at the screen. It was a picture of five kids—

a couple of them looked nine or ten years old—standing in front of a factory.

"Those kids look like they need a school more than they need a lawyer."

"The only way they'll ever get to school is if they had a good lawyer. They're all factory workers."

"I've heard about things like that," she said.

"I'd heard things too, but nothing like what I've read. Kids, as young as five and six, basically used as slave labor. They get paid next to nothing, if they even get paid at all. They're locked in factories, separated from their families, beaten and abused if they don't make quotas, or even if they do."

"Have you looked at the laws to protect them?" she asked.

"In some countries there are no laws, or if there are laws, they're so different from ours. It's legal for little kids to work twelve hours a day. It's legal to pay them next to nothing. And even the laws that are in place are ignored or broken. There are almost no health or safety codes either.

Some of the conditions are hazardous, dangerous and deadly."

"Some people say that at least they get some pay and enough food to survive. It's unfortunate and sad, but better than the alternative," she said.

"Maybe the alternative is to pay their parents enough so their kids wouldn't have to work."

"That sounds like a good alternative."

"All the companies have to do is earn less than fifteen billion dollars profit or pay the celebrities less than thirty million dollars to endorse the products."

"Or if people were prepared to pay more for the product," she said.

"That would work if people weren't so cheap."

"That is working. Have you heard about fair-trade products?" she asked.

"No." I typed the words *fair trade* into the search engine.

"It's products, often coffee or chocolate and clothes, which are guaranteed to be produced in conditions that are—"

"'Fair to the people who make them,'" I said, reading off the screen.

"Exactly."

"They pay them living wages, it says."

"And the factories or fields are more humane. Of course that means the product costs more."

"How much more?" I asked.

"We buy fair-trade coffee," she said, "and it's about an extra dollar per package."

"That's not too much."

"It's fair to both the producer and the consumer. Those that make it and those of us who buy it."

"So how do you know if something is fair trade?" I asked.

"Usually they advertise it. The real question is, how do we know that it really is fair trade?"

"That's the problem I'm having. I'm trying to figure out, for sure, what the truth is," I said.

"They used to say 'Believe only half of what you read' and that 'Seeing is believing.'"

"With photoshopping, that doesn't even work anymore. I could make a photograph of me working in one of these factories."

"So what do you believe?" she asked.

"I believe the reports from reputable organizations, like these ones," I said. I clicked up a report on child labor.

"Interesting," my mother said. "And how do you know that the report hasn't been altered or doctored?"

"Well...I guess I don't."

"A judgment always has to be made. And speaking of judgments, I better get back to work." She reached down and gave me a kiss on the top of head. "Not too much later, okay?"

"You neither."

"Promise."

It was time for me to go to sleep. I wasn't going to solve the problems of the world right now. I went to turn off the computer but hesitated. I was partway through the special report on child labor. I'd just finish it.

I scrolled down the page to where I'd left off. It was a list of the worst offenders, the companies that year after year were the worst exploiters of children, the ten biggest bottom-feeders. This wasn't going to be good bedtime reading, but who was I to complain? I had a bed and a roof over my head, and tomorrow I'd go to school, not some sweatshop.

chapter nine

Oswald and I stood at the double doors of the gym and watched. It was sort of fascinating. The gym looked like a gigantic cut-rate clothing store. There were dozens and dozens of tables filled with the items that made up the school uniforms. There were mirrors and dividers to make mini-change rooms all over the gym. There were also twenty or thirty employees of the uniform company taking measurements, getting clothes for kids and working the cash registers.

Wandering among the tables were the students about to be fitted. They were going grade by grade. We were next. By the end of the day, it was all supposed to be done—an impressive act of organization.

Oswald was, of course, in his uniform. He seemed to enjoy wearing it. I thought that he would hate the uniform. Oswald prided himself on being different. I guess being the only one in a uniform made him an individual. Everybody had been watching him, asking him questions and checking out his clothes. I knew him well enough to know that he wouldn't like it nearly as much once everybody was in a matching costume.

"Looks like you're just dying to get in there and get fitted."

It was Julia.

"Can you blame him?" Oswald asked. "This look is nothing short of sharp."

"Strawberry jam and toast," Julia replied.

Oswald looked confused. That wasn't the response I'd been expecting either.

She pointed to a stain on his jacket. "You had strawberry jam and toast for breakfast."

Oswald tapped his finger against the stain and then popped it in his mouth. "Raspberry jam. And the beauty of the polyester blend is that it doesn't stain permanently. I could spread jam directly on the material and it would just wipe away."

"Another fine reason why we should all wear uniforms," she replied sarcastically.

"I think this thing is practically fireproof," he added.

"Why don't we try to set it on fire and find out!" she said with mock excitement.

Julia was surrendering the idea that she could stop the uniform. She'd found that while lots of people were unhappy about them, nobody was willing to do anything about it. Not that there was much to be done.

It was a board initiative, supported by the parents' association, and it was something that Mr. Roberts wanted. That was a deadly combination.

"I think whether you like the uniforms or not, it's a done deal," I said.

"It's a shame that nobody came up with a great idea to stop them," she said.

Of course that comment was aimed straight at me. I hadn't come up with an idea. Not that I had been thinking that hard, or cared that much, but if I had I would have told her—probably.

"You really are okay with this, aren't you?" she said, looking me square in the eye.

"It's not a big deal," I said.

"It's not a big deal to you."

I'd had just about enough. "It shouldn't be a big deal to anybody."

"And what is that supposed to mean?" she demanded.

"Look, Jules, after what we've been studying in our social justice class, how can you get so upset about stupid uniforms?"

"Hah, do you know why we've been studying all those child labor issues right now?" she asked.

"Because it isn't phys ed, and those are social justice topics?" I suggested.

"Mr. Roberts is trying to distract you with those issues so you don't think about the school uniforms, that's why."

"Are you serious? Do you really think that's what he's been doing?"

"It's his style, just like the way he didn't consult anybody and ambushed us with it."

"It is his style to not consult. It isn't his style to be sneaky."

"Yeah, defend him like a good little soldier."

I felt like telling her that the wedding was definitely not going to happen, but that would have been too confusing and embarrassing.

"I'm going to go get fitted now," I said. "You should probably come in too. After all, you can't burn it in protest unless you have it."

"Funny, very funny, but I think I have better places to go and better people to be with."

She turned and walked away.

"She's a lot madder at you than she is at me," Oswald said. "And do you know why?"

"Why?" I asked, although I was pretty sure I didn't want to hear his answer.

"High expectations," he said.

"And that means?"

"She doesn't expect me to care or come up with an answer, so she's only mildly annoyed with me. But you? She thinks you might be able to come up with a solution. You've set the bar too high. That's why she's mad at you."

That did make sense.

"Well, that and the fact that she's still interested in dating you someday," Oswald added.

"And why do you think that?"

He tapped the side of his head. "Great intelligence combined with a keen sense of the human condition."

"Yeah, right."

"Don't believe me. You wouldn't be the first person to doubt greatness. Do you know how many people thought Galileo was crazy, but he showed them when he discovered gravity."

"Galileo didn't discover gravity. That was Newton. Galileo discovered that the planets circle the sun."

"And what do you think holds them up there, fishing wire?"

"Thanks for the lesson on the universe. I better go and get fitted."

Oswald followed me into the gym. There was rack after rack of jackets. I looked through them for one that was my size. The material was stiff and coarse to the touch. Oswald said his jacket softened with wear.

I looked at the size. It was large—my size. The tag listed the material blend and washing instructions. The whole jacket could just go in the washing machine. On the inside pocket was a symbol. Strange—that symbol looked very familiar to me. I wondered if I'd seen it on Oswald's jacket, or maybe I owned something made by them or...No, that wasn't it. I remembered. But that couldn't be right...could it?

chapter ten

"Do you see this label?" I asked Oswald, as I held the jacket directly in front of his face.

"Be a little hard to miss," he said as he pushed it aside.

"But do you know what it means?" I asked.

"Like I said before, it's a polyester blend, machine washable, and—"

"No, no, the symbol. That *is* the name of the company."

"Why would they use a symbol instead of a name?" Oswald asked.

"Partially so they don't have to use translations or different types of writing in other countries, but I think mainly so people won't know who they are. It's to confuse people."

"Well, it's working. I'm confused. But why wouldn't they want people to know the name of the company? Do they make bad stuff?"

"Because then people will know that they were made by a company that...wait...we need to check the others to see if they're all made by the same company. Maybe it just some of them." I tossed the jacket onto a pile of other clothes.

I started sorting through the jackets. I grabbed one from the hanger and threw it open to reveal the label. There was the symbol. I tossed it onto the table. I grabbed the next—there it was again—and threw it aside. The next and the next...all had that innocent-looking symbol. Maybe it was just the jackets.

"The sweaters all have it too," Oswald said.

I went over to the next table and started looking at the items there—they were skirts. I opened up a skirt—that was a new experience—and searched for the label. There it was again. I threw it aside to check a second and then a third, and each had the same label.

"Excuse me!" a woman called out. "I don't think those skirts are for you!"

I threw the skirt onto the pile.

"And there is no need for you to make a mess here!" she scolded.

"Sorry...I'm really sorry."

I turned away and went over to the table that was piled high with pants. Each and every one was labeled the same.

I grabbed Oswald by the jacket. "Come with me. I have to find Mr. Roberts and tell him about this."

"I think he knows about the uniforms being here and the fittings taking place. He's quick that way," Oswald said.

"Not that. I have to tell him about the manufacturer. I have to show him the label and...wait...no...I have to show him information about the label. We have to go to the resource center."

"I'm not allowed there," Oswald said.

"What?"

"A minor misunderstanding about missing books and fines that haven't been paid. And even more unbelievable, something about how I made too much noise. Let's go to the computer lab instead."

"Wherever. As long as there's a computer and Internet access, I'm good."

We left the gym and hurried down the hall.

"What exactly do you need the Internet for?" Oswald asked.

"You'll see soon enough."

There was no class in the computer lab, and more than half of the machines were available. I sat down and quickly logged in. The machine whirred and purred but didn't seem to want to move very quickly. Finally a search engine came on and I typed in the address. It popped up, the heading on the page simple but clear—*The Ten*

Worst Offenders. And right below that, in third place, was that awful symbol!

I printed the page as Oswald read over my shoulder. I didn't have to read it because I knew exactly what it said.

"You know, just because it's on the Internet doesn't mean it's true," Oswald said.

"Look at the source."

He scrolled down the page. "Okay, so this is a good source, but maybe it's an old report and they've changed."

"Look at the date at the top," I said.

He went back up to the top. It had been published earlier this year.

"That still doesn't mean they haven't changed," he suggested.

"Maybe they have. Probably they haven't."

I logged out of the computer and went over to the printer and grabbed the sheet.

"We need to find Julia and tell her about this," Oswald said.

"Are you insane?" I asked.

"The jury is still out on that one," he joked. "But she is student president, and she does hate these uniforms and—"

"This would send her over the edge!" I said.

"Wouldn't that be fun to watch?" Oswald asked.

I grabbed him by his jacket. "You have to promise me you won't talk to Julia about this. That you won't talk to anybody about this...well, except for Mr. Roberts."

"What? I can only talk to the one person I don't want to talk to?"

"We have to," I said. "He has to know about this."

"Then you tell him. You don't need me there."

"I need to show him the label on your jacket."

Oswald pulled off his jacket and tried to hand it to me.

"What are you doing?" I asked. "Just come with me."

"Nope. I'm not going near him."

"It sounds like you're afraid to go."

"I am afraid and so should you be," Oswald said.

"Afraid of what?" I demanded.

"Haven't you ever heard the saying they kill the messenger?"

"He's not going to kill us."

"It's not *us*, it's *me* I'm worried about. You he likes."

"He likes you too."

"He likes me, but he really likes you," Oswald said.

"Look, he's not going to kill us," I said. "He's never killed anybody before."

"Are you sure? He was in the Marines."

"Regardless, he's never killed a student. You know him. He's tough, but he is fair. He'll want to hear this."

Oswald took a deep breath. "I'll go with you, but I still think this is a mistake."

chapter eleven

Mr. Roberts sat at his desk reading the report I'd brought him. I could feel sweat pouring down from my armpits. Oswald was so silent and still that I almost forgot he was there. I think he wanted to blend into the background so he wouldn't be noticed by Mr. Roberts.

Mr. Roberts looked up from the report. "This company has a very poor record."

"Not just poor. It's one of the worst in the world," I said.

"I'm very glad you brought this to my attention," Mr. Roberts said.

I felt like giving Oswald a nudge. He was so worried that we'd be in trouble that—

"We thought you'd want to know," Oswald said.

Now I felt like making that nudge into a punch.

"I do appreciate it," Mr. Roberts said. "But to be honest with you, I found out about this myself just a few days ago."

"You did?"

"It was very distressing," Mr. Roberts said. "I was very upset."

"It is upsetting. It's terrible!" I exclaimed.

"I agree completely. Now if you'll excuse me I have a lot of work to do."

He got to his feet and so did we. We shook hands. I was glad we told him. It was the right thing to do.

"There's so much I have to do to take care of these uniforms," said Mr. Roberts.

I could just imagine the phone calls he'd have to make to cancel them and how upset people might be.

"I hope we can get all the uniforms distributed so that everybody will be wearing them by Monday," he said.

"What?" I gasped. "We're still going to be wearing the uniforms?"

"Unfortunately, yes, starting Monday as scheduled."

"But...but...they're made in a sweatshop... by child labor," I sputtered.

"Yes, it is unfortunate that they were not made by a more reputable company."

"Almost every company in the world is more reputable!" I snapped. "There's only two that are worse, and they don't make clothes!"

"So what do you suggest we do?" Mr. Roberts asked.

"I think we should get uniforms from another company."

"The board has a contract with this company to supply the uniforms. They've been paid for and delivered before anybody knew anything about this."

"Then maybe we should forget the uniforms and stay with regular clothes," I said.

"We can't do that either."

"Why not? You're the principal. You run the school. Just say we don't have to wear uniforms!" I exclaimed.

"It isn't that simple," said Mr. Roberts.

"Sure it is. Just pick up the microphone and make an announcement."

"Ian, this decision was made at the board level, by my bosses. I have no choice."

"But...but...but..." I had no idea what more to say.

"Boys, I want you to know that I have pursued this to the top level of the board, and I've been assured that this company will never be used again."

"But we're still going to have to use them, have to wear them this year, regardless?" I asked.

He nodded his head. "I fully appreciate how difficult, how confusing, how unsettling this must be, but there is no choice."

"There are always choices!" I snapped.

He got up and circled around his desk and sat down on the edge right in front of us.

"I want to tell you boys that I'm pleased— no, more than that—proud of you for wanting to take a stand against this, but you can't. I've been told that students or staff that do not wear the uniforms will be suspended."

"I'm not afraid of a suspension," I said.

"Maybe you should be," Mr. Roberts said. "You've been suspended once before. A second suspension on your file could really affect your ability to get into a good university."

I didn't know what to say. I didn't think it was fair or right for us to wear these uniforms—but...

"I think you both know that I have high regard for you. I only want what's best for you. And because of that I'm going to ask you to do me two favors."

"What do you want us to do?" I asked.

"I want you to do nothing. First off, don't tell anybody, and second, please do not try to do anything about it. Can I have your word on that?"

"Sure, that works for me," Oswald replied.

I didn't answer.

"Ian?"

"I don't want to give my word if I don't know that I can keep it." I got up to leave.

"Ian, I don't want you to do anything rash. I don't want to have to punish you, but you know that I'll do whatever I have to do," Mr. Roberts said.

"I understand that," I said. "And maybe I have to do what I have to do."

I walked out the door. I'd only gone a few feet when Oswald caught up to me.

"Okay, this is going to sound strange, especially coming from me, but don't do anything stupid," he said.

"I didn't say I was going to do anything," I replied.

"But you didn't say you *weren't*. How about if we both agree that we don't tell Julia anything about this? She would go crazy!"

"Maybe we should tell her!"

"That wasn't a suggestion. That was a warning. What good would it do to tell her?"

"Okay, maybe you're right...maybe...maybe not...I don't know what we should do."

"Who says we have to do anything?" Oswald asked. "The only people who know about this are me, you and Mr. Roberts. I don't think he's going to be telling anybody. If we keep our mouths shut, who's going to know?"

I didn't know what to say to that—in one way he wasn't wrong, but in another way he was *completely* wrong because *I* knew. Why did I look at that website, why did I notice who made the uniforms? Being ignorant and innocent would have been so much easier.

"Let's just keep it to ourselves for right now," Oswald suggested. "My mother says you can't un-tell something once you've said it."

"That's good advice."

"Yeah. I'll even try to practice it myself this time."

"I just didn't expect that reaction from Mr. Roberts," I said.

"Neither did I, but really, what did you think he'd do?" Oswald asked.

"I thought he'd cancel the uniforms."

The PA crackled to life. There was going to be an announcement.

"*Could I have your attention, please!*" Mr. Roberts said.

We stopped moving. Everybody in the hall stood still.

"*I have an announcement to make about the school uniforms. Due to some supply issues,*" Mr. Roberts continued, "*it may be that not every student will have a complete school uniform by Monday. Every student and staff member will have received a jacket and tie. It is expected that everyone will wear those items. Any student or staff member not in a uniform on Monday morning will not be admitted to the building and will be subject to a one-day suspension. No exceptions. Thank you and have a good afternoon.*"

Oswald and I looked at each other. There was no doubt. He knew, he understood, and he'd decided to ignore the whole thing.

But could I ignore it?

Julia always gave me a hard time that Mr. Roberts was my hero. Maybe in some ways he *had* been. Things change.

chapter twelve

I slipped outside, quietly closing the door behind me. My parents had gone to bed, and I didn't want to wake them. They would want to know where I was going at eleven thirty at night, and I didn't have an answer. I didn't know where I was going, but I needed to walk to try to clear my head. If I told them that, they would have wanted to know what was cluttering it, and I didn't want to tell them. I hadn't told anybody. Not Julia, not my parents, nobody. Oswald had sworn to do the same. Oswald and I had talked about it a lot, but that hadn't lead to answers, just more confusion.

I walked along trying to make sense of what had happened. Or, I guess, what hadn't happened. Oswald had told me that I'd expected too much from Mr. Roberts. He was right. I had expected something. He was the principal. He had taught us so much about social justice and becoming global citizens, about thinking globally and acting locally. Now it was more like *think globally, do nothing locally*.

I felt so disappointed—in him for doing nothing and in me for not coming up with a plan. I guess it wasn't realistic to think Mr. Roberts would cancel the uniforms—that he *could* cancel the uniforms.

It was cool, and I started to feel sprinkles coming from the sky. Great, it was going to start raining. If I started home right now, I could avoid getting completely soaked. I didn't need to feel as miserable on the outside as I did on the inside. When I got home maybe I could talk to my parents

about the whole thing...no, not tonight...
They were asleep, and I wasn't going to
wake them. Calling Oswald would mean
just rehashing the same things again.

That left Julia. Should I call her? Once
I told her, there was no way of getting the
genie back into the bottle. She was like an
avalanche, and once it started downhill
nothing could stop it...stop it from doing
what though? I didn't have any better
answer now than I did three hours or three
days or three weeks ago. The uniforms were
going to happen, and it didn't matter where
or how they were made.

I was almost directly in front of our
school. It was completely dark except for
one window at the front of the building...
was that Mr. Roberts's office? He couldn't
be in there working, could he? He did say
he had a lot to do.

I cut across the grass, and at that same
instant the rain started to come down
more heavily. The storm made the dark
seem darker and the light coming from the
window brighter.

It was definitely his office. I could tell by the big Dr. Martin Luther King quote on the wall—*Injustice anywhere is a threat to justice everywhere*. It was Mr. Roberts's office, but was he there? He may have left the lights on, or the caretaker was cleaning his office.

I crept through the bushes outside the window. I peeked in and—Mr. Roberts was sitting at his desk, working. He looked up, saw me and startled!

His expression changed from shocked to familiar as he recognized me. He motioned toward the front door. "Go around," he mouthed.

I waved and then headed for the door. It was—of course—locked, but at least I was out of the rain. Mr. Roberts came into the foyer. He walked over and pushed open the door.

"You startled me," he said.

"Sorry. I was just out walking and saw the light on and came over to see."

"I was startled, but I wasn't surprised," he said.

"You expected me to come here?"

"I expected you to be troubled by what we talked about today."

I nodded.

"You don't understand why I'm not doing anything about the uniforms."

Again I nodded.

"It might be different if the uniforms had been my idea to begin with," he said.

"They weren't your idea?"

"No. They were the idea of some committee up at the board office. They see uniforms as a way of creating discipline and bringing order to a school."

"You don't think they do that?" I asked.

"Do you think a marine is a marine only because of the uniform they wear?" he asked.

"Of course not."

"Because if all they needed was a uniform, you'd just send recruits to a tailor instead of putting them through advanced training and giving them continual drills. That's what makes a marine."

"And you think the same thing about a good student," I said.

"Good students and good schools are brought about by planning and caring, and by having good teachers and good administration and good policies. Uniforms are just window dressing, an excuse to not do the things that really matter."

"So you're against uniforms?"

"Never liked them and never wanted them."

"But we're getting them," I said.

"That was the order I was given, that we would have uniforms," he said.

"But couldn't you have just said no?" I asked.

"A good marine follows orders."

"You're not a marine anymore."

"But I am employed by this board of education. It's my role to implement their policies."

"Including the ones you don't agree with?" I asked.

He didn't answer right away. "Those are the policies that challenge us." He paused. "Especially this one. After I discovered who manufactured the uniforms, I brought it to the attention of my superiors. I told them the history of the company. I said a lot of the same things you said to me."

"And it didn't do any good," I said.

He shook his head.

"They are not prepared to make any changes." He paused. "I shouldn't have told you that. That was inappropriate. You better get home. I'll see you Monday morning."

"Sure, good night...wait...I have one more question."

"Go ahead."

"If anybody refuses to wear the uniforms, they will be suspended, right?"

"Any student or staff not in uniform will be denied entry to the school and will receive a one-day suspension."

"And if they show up without a uniform the next day?" I asked.

"Three-day suspension."

"And if they show up after that without a uniform?"

"A two-week suspension," he said. "And the next offence would be an expulsion."

I shook my head. "It just doesn't seem right. If we decide to boycott the uniforms, to do the things we've been taught—the things *you* taught us—we'll be punished."

"In some ways it is completely fair," he said. "If you choose to break a rule or law and you know the consequence, then receiving that consequence is fair."

"Even if the rule is wrong?" I asked.

"Gandhi and Dr. King didn't act because they thought there would be no consequence. They knew what could happen, what would happen, but they went ahead anyway. That's what made them great leaders," Mr. Roberts said. "It's late and it's raining even harder. Do you want me to drive you home?"

"Thanks for the offer," I said, "but I think I need to walk." I had even more things to think about now.

I headed back out into the rain. I was already soaked, so I wasn't going to get any wetter. Besides, I wasn't going home. I had one more stop to make.

chapter thirteen

I stood on the steps with Oswald and Julia. There were dozens and dozens of other people out there with us. Everybody, including us, was wearing the new uniforms. Most of the people around us were just killing time before they had to go inside. That was pretty common. Others were starting to go inside. Mr. Roberts and a couple of the teachers—all of them in uniforms—were at the door, checking to make sure the students were in uniform.

"What time is it?" Oswald asked.

"Ten to nine," I said. "Ten minutes until we have to go inside."

Oswald looked nervous. "You know you don't have to do this," I said to him. "You can go in."

"I could, but I won't. I just hope it's not going to be only the three of us."

"It won't," I assured him. "You know that."

"I know," Oswald said.

"There will be at least twenty-three people involved," Julia said.

That was the number of students in our social justice class. Once Julia and I had talked on Friday night—well I guess it was really Saturday morning—we figured it was best to start with our class. We contacted all of them, and they all agreed that after what we'd been taught, there was no way we could walk into school wearing the uniforms.

"You know, Ian, if you had gotten onside with this earlier, there could have been way more people involved," Julia said.

"I told you almost as soon as I found out," I said. "The same day."

"But you knew about the uniform for weeks."

"This isn't about the uniforms."

"Of course it is!"

"No," I said. "It's about the uniforms being made under unfair conditions. If these uniforms were made by a company that did business responsibly I'd be walking into school today."

"I still think that—"

"There's a news crew!" Oswald said, pointing to the street.

We'd contacted a couple of TV stations and the local newspapers about what was going to happen. The only way any of this made sense was if people knew about it, and the press was the best way to get the word out.

"And here comes Roberts," Julia said.

Mr. Roberts was slowly descending the stairs. He could have been going anywhere, but I doubted it. He walked straight over to us and stopped in front of me.

"It's almost time for school to start," he said. "You three are in your uniforms. Can I assume you're going to be coming into the school?"

I shook my head, ever so slightly.

"I thought that might be the case," he said. "You know you'll be suspended."

"I know."

"No exceptions. Any student or staff not in school uniform will be suspended. In the case of staff, their pay would be withheld and they could possibly be dismissed."

"They'd be fired over this?" I asked.

"That is what I've been told," Mr. Roberts said. "The board will be even less sympathetic to staff than students. So, can you tell me exactly what is going to happen?"

Julia looked shocked. "I don't think—"

I reached over and touched her hand and offered a reassuring look.

"I won't try to stop you," Mr. Roberts said. "Even if I could. I just want to know what to expect."

Julia didn't look any less anxious. "It's okay," I said. "The first step I've already mentioned. When the bell goes we're not going inside. Instead we're going to take off the uniforms."

"And how many students are going to join you?"

"We don't know for sure," I admitted.

"Could it be only three?"

"It could be hundreds," Julia said.

"But we know we have at least twenty-three," I said.

"Every single person in our social justice class," Julia said.

"Everybody?" Mr. Roberts asked.

"Well...everybody except you," I said.

His expression faltered—like I'd struck him—but he quickly returned to his usual stoic look.

"Remember that social justice club you wanted to start?" I said. "I started it."

"I guess I should be complimenting you on your leadership skills."

"I had some help. Julia contacted the media and thought a press conference would be a good thing."

"Getting the word out. Very wise," he said.

"You taught us that was important," I reminded him.

"And next?" Mr. Roberts asked.

"We're going to do a protest march," I said.

"We're walking to the board office to ask to meet with the director of education to formally present our objection to the uniforms," Julia added.

"And if he won't meet with you?" Mr. Roberts asked.

"Then the press will be there to see that," I said.

"That he doesn't have time for his own students," Julia said. "I think he'd be an idiot to refuse to meet with us."

"Perhaps. Just try to avoid using that word or any other negative terms," Mr. Roberts cautioned.

"We'll be very respectful," I replied.

Mr. Roberts nodded slowly. He looked like he was thinking things through.

"And you are prepared to get suspended for a day, correct?"

"We all know the consequences," Julia said defiantly.

"And if the board doesn't agree to your demands, are you prepared to be suspended, again, for longer tomorrow?"

"We are," Julia snapped.

She sounded confident. Oswald didn't look so confident.

"And all of the other students, are they prepared to take a three-day suspension, or two weeks or even an expulsion?"

"We can't speak for anybody else," I said.

"Are you prepared?" he asked.

"I'm prepared to do what's right. That's what you taught us, what you talked to me about...doing the right thing even when there's the possibility of something bad happening."

"Ian, this isn't a *possibility*. This is a *certainty*," Mr. Roberts said.

"I'm prepared," I said. "Can I ask you a question?"

"Of course."

"When you showed us that YouTube clip,

when we had all those discussions in class, did you know who made the uniforms?"

"No, it wasn't until a few days later," he said.

"If you knew, would you have shown us that clip?" I asked.

"Yes, of course."

"Even though it could lead to us doing this?"

"If I compromised what I taught you, then I wouldn't be much of a teacher, would I?" he said. "I wanted you to know the—"

He was silenced by the bell.

"It's time for us all to do what we have to do," Mr. Roberts said.

He started up the stairs.

"So," I said. "We're really going to do this...right?"

"Not exactly a quote that would make Gandhi or Dr. King proud, but good enough," Julia said.

I took off my jacket, and pulled off my tie over my head as Julia and Oswald and kids all around us did the same. There were a lot more than twenty-three people. The stairs were covered with students.

On the sidewalk below, a camera crew was already filming the scene on the steps. It was time to tell people why we were doing this. Maybe some of them wouldn't understand or agree. Maybe my parents would be among them.

I looked up at the steps and caught Mr. Roberts's eye. He smiled and nodded his head ever so slightly, giving me a look of approval that maybe nobody else saw. He was telling me I was doing the right thing. And that's all that mattered.

Eric Walters is no stranger to social justice issues. His book *When Elephants Fight* (co-written by Adrian Bradbury) takes on the subject of the effect of wars on children, and *War of the Eagles* and *Caged Eagles* are novels about Japanese internment in British Columbia. A passionate literacy advocate, Eric enjoys visiting schools to talk about the power of books. Eric lives in Mississauga, Ontario.